NEW YORK REVIEW BOOKS
ILLUSTRATED BY ROGER DUVOISIN

Donkey-donkey
Written by Roger Duvoisin

The Frog in the Well
Written by Alvin Tresselt

THE HOUSE
OF
FOUR SEASONS

by Roger Duvoisin

THE NEW YORK REVIEW CHILDREN'S COLLECTION, NEW YORK

THIS IS A NEW YORK REVIEW BOOK
PUBLISHED BY THE NEW YORK REVIEW OF BOOKS
435 Hudson Street, New York, NY 10014
www.nyrb.com

A catalog record for this book is available from the Library of Congress

ISBN 978-1-68137-098-9
Available as an electronic book, ISBN 978-1-68137-099-6

Cover design by Louise Fili Ltd.

Manufactured in China
1 2 3 4 5 6 7 8 9 10

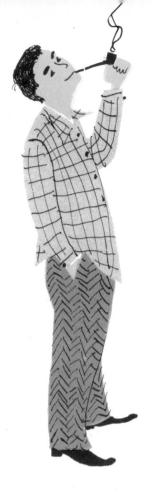

Father

Mother

Billy

Suzy

Drove out one sunny day to buy a house in the country.
Along the winding lanes,
they saw many houses with signs FOR SALE

But they liked best an old house which sat quietly among the tall weeds listening to the birds singing in the tree tops.

It was a very old house. The shutters were hanging this way and that, the stairs were tumbling upon one another, the rain pipes had rusted away, and an old owl lived in the attic.

"The old owl is wise," said Father.
"He chose a nice house. Let's choose it too."

Soon there was much hustle and bustle
around the old house.
The carpenter hung the shutters tight,
the mason rebuilt the stairs, the tinsmith came
with new rain pipes. But the old owl, who could not sleep
with so much noise, flew away to find a new home.

"The house needs painting, too," said Father.
"Wouldn't it be fun to paint it ourselves?"

"Yes," cried Suzy, "let's paint it red with green shutters.
It would be beautiful in the spring
with all the flowers and the buds on the trees!"

"No, yellow with purple shutters," cried Billy.
"It would be so bright in summertime
when everything turns green.

"Red and yellow are beautiful colors," said Mother,
"but I think a brown house with blue shutters
would be more handsome in the fall
with all the yellow leaves that flutter all around."

Father laughed. "How about a green house
with orange shutters for winter?
It would be so gay—like a Christmas tree in the snow!"

"Well," said Mother, "Imagine a blue, red, yellow,
purple, green, orange, brown house!
It would look like grandmother's bed quilt."

But Suzy clapped her hands and cried,
"Let's paint each side a different color,
one side for each of us!"
"And one side for each season," cried Billy.
"We could call it the House of Four Seasons!"

"I never saw such a house," Father mused,
"but let's play with all those colors and see
how we like them."

And the next day, Father, Mother, Suzy and Billy
went to town to buy at the hardware store
a ladder, four brushes, and cans of red, blue,
yellow, brown, orange, purple, and green paint.

But the storekeeper said,
"Here are red, yellow and blue paint, but, I'm sorry,
we have no brown, no orange, no purple, no green."
"Oh!" cried Suzy, "then we can't have
our House of Four Seasons!"
"We can have the yellow house," said Billy.
"Or red," said Mother.
"Let's take home the blue, yellow and red," said Father.
"I'll show you what three colors can do."

"You'll see," said Father

when they were home,

"colors can do

many tricks when they get together."

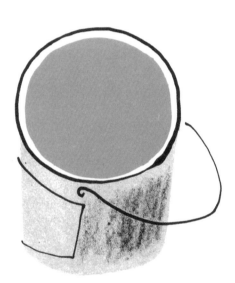

And Father took a brush

and dipped it in the yellow paint.

"What can the yellow and blue do when they meet?
Why they make green!
And so we have four colours instead of the original three."

"What trick will the red and yellow play
when they meet? See, they turn into orange!
And so we have five colors instead of three."

"And when the red and the blue cross each other's paths,
they change to purple.
And so we have six colors instead of three."

"And if the blue, the yellow and the red
meet at the same place, they turn into brown.
And so we have all the colors we wanted!"

"Then we *can* have the House of Four Seasons!" said Suzy.
"Wait," said Father, "I have an idea
for another sort of House of Four Seasons.
When we mix blue, red and yellow with the brush
they are brown. But when they mix another way,
they can do an even better trick."
Father painted a disk of heavy cardboard with the three colors.

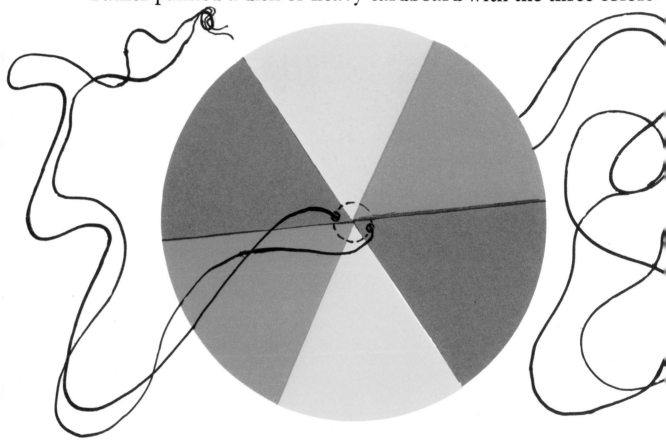

He put two strings through two holes near the center

and he began 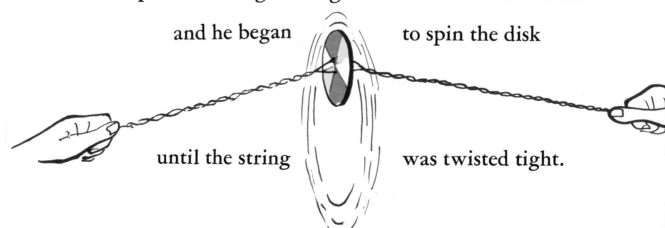 to spin the disk

until the string was twisted tight.

Then by first pulling on the string, then drawing it in,
he made it spin fast, very fast...until it buzzed.

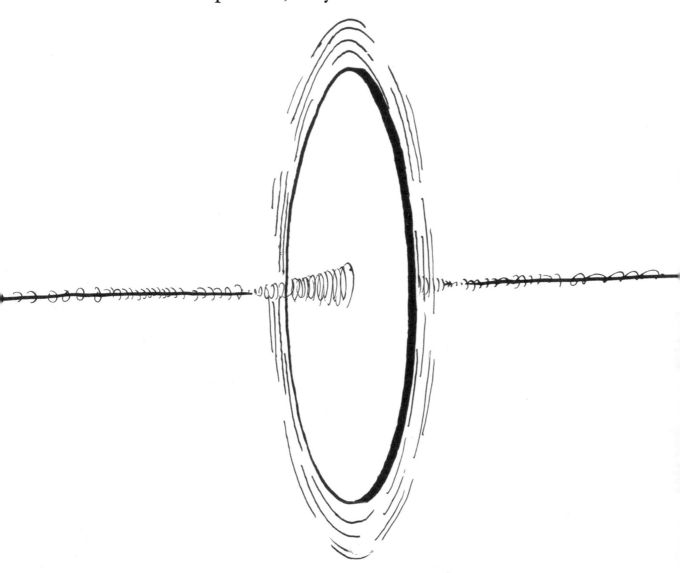

As the children watched, the red, blue and yellow
disappeared, and the disk became white.
"You see," said Father, "this trick shows
that white is made of all colors.
And now I think we have found the right color for our house.
Let's paint it white—since white *is* all colors.
It will make the true House of Four Seasons."

So Father, Mother, Suzy and Billy
put up ladders
all around the house
and painted it a fresh lovely white.

It was very beautiful,
and when it was all finished
the birds flew and sang in all the bushes.

And the old owl came back
to live in an old tree nearby.

ROGER DUVOISIN (1900–1980) was born in Geneva, Switzerland, and graduated from the École des Arts et Métiers and the École des Beaux-Arts. In the late 1920s, he immigrated to the United States, where he soon began writing and illustrating children's books. The author of more than forty of his own books, Duvoisin also collaborated with many writers, including his wife, Louise Fatio Duvoisin, and Alvin Tresselt, with whom he won a Caldecott Medal for *White Snow, Bright Snow* in 1948 and the Caldecott Honor Award for *Hide and Seek Fog* in 1966.

ELEANOR FARJEON
The Little Bookroom

PENELOPE FARMER
Charlotte Sometimes

PAUL GALLICO
The Abandoned

LEON GARFIELD
The Complete Bostock and Harris
Leon Garfield's Shakespeare Stories
Smith: The Story of a Pickpocket

RUMER GODDEN
An Episode of Sparrows
The Mousewife

MARIA GRIPE AND HARALD GRIPE
The Glassblower's Children

LUCRETIA P. HALE
The Peterkin Papers

RUSSELL AND LILLIAN HOBAN
The Sorely Trying Day

RUSSELL HOBAN AND QUENTIN BLAKE
The Marzipan Pig

RUTH KRAUSS AND MARC SIMONT
The Backward Day

DOROTHY KUNHARDT
Junket Is Nice
Now Open the Box

MUNRO LEAF AND ROBERT LAWSON
Wee Gillis

RHODA LEVINE AND EVERETT AISON
Arthur

RHODA LEVINE AND EDWARD GOREY
He Was There from the Day We Moved In
Three Ladies Beside the Sea

RHODA LEVINE AND KARLA KUSKIN
Harrison Loved His Umbrella

BETTY JEAN LIFTON AND EIKOH HOSOE
Taka-chan and I

ASTRID LINDGREN
Mio, My Son
Seacrow Island

NORMAN LINDSAY
The Magic Pudding

ERIC LINKLATER
The Wind on the Moon

J. P. MARTIN
Uncle
Uncle Cleans Up

JOHN MASEFIELD
The Box of Delights
The Midnight Folk

WILLIAM McCLEERY AND WARREN CHAPPELL
Wolf Story

JEAN MERRILL AND RONNI SOLBERT
The Elephant Who Liked to Smash Small Cars
The Pushcart War

E. NESBIT
The House of Arden

ALFRED OLLIVANT'S
Bob, Son of Battle: The Last Gray Dog of Kenmuir
A New Version by LYDIA DAVIS

DANIEL PINKWATER
Lizard Music

OTFRIED PREUSSLER
Krabat & the Sorcerer's Mill
The Little Water Sprite
The Little Witch
The Robber Hotzenplotz

VLADIMIR RADUNSKY AND CHRIS RASCHKA
Alphabetabum

ALASTAIR REID AND BOB GILL
Supposing…

ALASTAIR REID AND BEN SHAHN
Ounce Dice Trice

BARBARA SLEIGH
Carbonel and Calidor
Carbonel: The King of the Cats
The Kingdom of Carbonel